Arctic Threat

David G Evans

Table of Contents

15 years ago, up in the arctic, an alien species moved into the region. They lived in their special spacious spacecraft.

They came from a planet that was 2,000 light years away. Each day they would explore more areas of the arctic, while exploring a polar bear came after them.

They shot it with their special weapon, killing it. They continued their exploration of the area, and soon came to the end of the land.

Hundreds of walruses were lying together just waiting to jump into the water to take a swim. A norwal brought its head up out of the water, to observe what was going on above the water.

The sky darkened and a blizzard began, the aliens couldn't even see a foot in front of them. A few polar bears were looking for a place to shelter during the blizzard.

They couldn't find anywhere to shelter so they just stopped and laid down. The wind picked up to 35 mph, the aliens bodies still ran warm during the freezing temperatures.

It was just 10 degrees out there, the aliens brought out some kind of bright light from their coat pocket and now they could see where they were going much better. They came upon an abandoned shack and decided to see what was inside of it.

There was nothing inside that they wanted to look at, so they quickly exited. They brought out 2 timed bombs and stuck them on the sides of the shack, and quickly ran from it. 5 minutes later the shack exploded, throwing all kinds of debris all over the place.

Suddenly a geyser shot up where the shack used to be, the aliens were surprised to see a geyser up in the arctic. The aliens soon got tired out and looked for a place where they could camp out.

They sat in an area where there was thick pieces of ice that grew together, the aliens brought out 2 heating pods.

They set the pods temperatures at 75 degrees, they kept their eyes out for any wildlife that may come and bother them.

An hour later the blizzard stopped, the aliens got tired of resting, and packed up their heating pods and continued there adventure. The thick pieces of ice began to vibrate, cracks began to form in the thick ice block.

The ice block began warming up and began its melting process. The massive ice block broke open, and 2 arctic guardians got up from the ice. They smashed through the ice with their mighty fists, to retrieve their fire swords. Their job is to drive out any other worldly aliens or evil beings out of the arctic.

They became frozen when they fought with the ice monster, that used a spell to put tons of ice on top of them.

Eventually the aliens found their way back to their spacecraft, and settled in. When the animals saw the guardians they felt safe and secure. After walking for quite a while, the guardians came upon a heard of muskox.

2 of the 5 muskox's began fighting between one another, they slammed into each other's heads three times before giving up the fight and resting.

One of the muskox became annoyed when an arctic fox walked past it. The muskox chased after the fox but was never able to catch up to it.

It turned around and headed back to the herd and rested. The guardians soon came to where the water met the land, they saw the dorsal fin of an orca going past them.

It was searching the waters for its prey the ringed seal and the harp seal. Nearby to the orca there were several walruses, some of the walruses went into the water.

The orca knew not to go after them because they put up such a fight. It fought with a walrus some years ago and has a scar on its side from it.

It turned away from where the walruses were and returned to searching for its prey. A few Greenland sharks swam past the orca, both predators get along well for the most part.

The Greenland sharks are slow movers and outlive most shark species and have a backbone. The orca came to open waters and witnessed a mother beluga whale with her calf.

When the beluga whale mother saw the orca she quickly got closer to her calf to assure that it was safe from the predators lurking nearby.

Meanwhile on land the guardians, we're on the move. A bald eagle flew over to one of the guardians and landed on his shoulder.

A stoat also known as a weasel came up out of his burrow when it saw the guardians, it followed behind them. The bald eagle spotted the stoat but didn't go after it because it had eaten just a few minutes ago.

Soon afterwards the stoat ran off. Just up ahead of the guardians was a sheer cliff, there were many puffin nests on the side of the cliff.

Only a few puffins remained in their nests, while the rest of them had flown away looking for food. There were 2 mother puffins, with their young which are called pufflings.

The guardians watched as one of the puffins nests almost slipped off the cliff. They were ready to save the nest if need be, they headed away from the cliff and went East.

As they pushed on further they spotted a large herd of reindeer, there were 3 calves in the herd who were standing beside their mothers.

Most of the adult reindeer were grazing on the grass, but one of the reindeer got spooked and ran away from the herd.

Nearby a snowy owl spotted 2 rodents and took flight to go after them. After landing it was easily able to catch its prey, after eating it's fill, it flew off in search of more rodents to consume.

The eagle remained perched on the guardian's shoulder, observing the area around it. It was so content that it almost fell asleep.

Off to the left of the guardians were several arctic hares walking around, looking for vegetation to eat. There was a young hare that was wandering away from the other hares, they came over to it and stayed with it.

Chapter 1

When the guardians took their next step the eagle flew off one of their shoulders, it must have sensed danger and it was right.

The guardians saw the spacecraft and proceeded towards it with great caution. They knew that at any minute aliens could come out of it and attack them. They held their swords firmly in their hands, waiting there patiently for their enemy to show itself.

Both aliens were getting their things ready to take another trip, they made sure that their weapons were working well.

They opened the spacecraft and when they walked out, the first thing that they saw were the guardians, holding their fire swords.

Both aliens began firing their weapons at both guardians, but it was no match for the guardians heightened reflexes.

They easily dodged each projectile fired at them and used their swords as shields in some instances.

The aliens weapons overheated and could no longer be fired. A blue orb formed in the hands of one of the aliens and threw it at the guardians. The guardians backed away and when the blue orb hit the ground it violently exploded causing millions of volts of electricity to pass through the ground in front of them. They immediately went into their fighting stances and swung at the aliens with their swords.

The aliens were slower than they anticipated they would be, they swung their swords a certain way and a large fireball came from the swords and went towards the aliens, but the aliens dodged the fireball.

The other guardian came after them from their right side, in their concerted efforts they hit both aliens with their swords killing them.

After killing the aliens, they went to work destroying the spacecraft with their swords. They touched the spacecraft with their swords causing it to catch fire.

But they still weren't finished, the thought of defeating the ice monster was still very much in the back of their minds.

They began their trek to where the ice monster dwells, it took them 3 hours to get to the summit of where the monster dwells. They would have to climb a mountain to get to the monster, but this was no difficulty for them.

After a while later they climbed over the mountain, they observed the ice monster from afar.

One time they came face to face with the ice monsters, army of death hawks that are the size of a dragon. The ice monster was sitting on his ice throne, just looking around.

Both guardians charged after the ice monster, luckily they caught him by surprise and immediately went into combat with him.

It didn't take them long at all to overpower him, they swung their swords at him at the same time breaking him into two killing him.

They were feeling so accomplished at this point, there wings came out of their backs and they flew away up into space and returned to their home planet.

From that day forward no aliens never moved into the arctic again. 2 years after this incident, all the polar bears in the arctic died off, because of complications from climate change.

2 massive ice caps melted raising the sea level by 7%, however the population of arctic hare population exploded to over 30,000 hares.

32% more grass was growing in the arctic, allowing the hares to eat their fill and have many offspring. This meant that there was plenty of prey for the arctic fox, causing their population to almost double.

This caused a 10% decrease in the population of stouts but wouldn't cause them to go extinct. A 3rd of the population of the harp seals became sickened from a certain kind of bacteria.

After 15 days of being sickened they died. The Ptarmigan population rose by 19% and the snow goose population is slightly rising.

The next day up in the arctic, there was a curious reindeer that got too close to a bull moose's domain. The moose became unsettled and charged after the reindeer.

The reindeer turned and quickly ran the other way, as the moose was walking back to its domain a polar bear came out of nowhere and attacked it from the side.

The moose fought back by giving the bear a swift kick to the chest, then it slammed into the bear with its cumbersome antlers.

The bear stood up on its back legs, and swung it's huge paw, hitting the moose square in the face. It's sharp claws dug into the side of the moose’s face and it let out a groan of agony.

A herd of muskox ran out of grass where they were grazing and went searching for more in a different area, close by to where the moose and bear were fighting.

The growls from the bear alerted the herd of muskox, one of the large male muskox walked away from the herd and charged down the hill at the polar bear and moose.

It rammed into the bears side with so much force that it caused it to let go of the moose. The moose took it’s chance to get away and ran.

The bear turned and was ready to stand up, when the muskox slammed into its hind legs. The bear let out a cry and limped away from the muskox.

Then the muskox joined back up with its herd and began grazing once again. Suddenly the ground began to shake, causing the animals to run for cover.

An arctic fox made a run for it back to its den. The shaking just lasted for 5 minutes, then stopped. The shaking caused something under the ice to awaken.

Rory and Eyana are microbiologists working for a company called advanced biology, there currently working together on an environmental project.

In the past they worked together on 6 projects, each project was difficult in its own way. On one of the projects, they were sent to Australia for three weeks, where they studied a new species of fish. They were studying it's odd pigmentation; the fishes entire body was lime green with white spots.

They found that these fish were more active at night than during the day and witnessed how these fish would bully the smaller fish by hitting them with their tail.

While the male fishes were larger than the female fishes. Their bodies are very agile, and we're able to pass through smaller areas by squeezing through them. They had many sharp teeth in their mouth and would sometimes go after fish larger than their size.

On their 2nd project they were sent to a remote region to study Greenland sharks. They were given one underwater drone, with 4 high-definition cameras, simply press a button and the cameras will change to night vision.

The cameras are mounted on either sides of it. It can stay under the water for 9 hours continuously, then it must be brought back to the surface to be recharged.

It takes just 2 hours to charge it back up to 100% and has a hefty price tag of $200,000. It can go speeds up to 65 miles per hour forward and 40 miles per hour in reverse and left to right.

After observing the Greenland sharks they learned that the sharks are able to catch prey while they're sleeping.

2 out of the 8 sharks that they observed had parasites living in 1 of their eyes, these parasites are called Ommatokoita elongata.

Oddly enough the parasite just chooses to live in one of the sharks eyes instead of living in both. They may be at the top of the food chain but are sometimes hunted by sperm whales.

There are no verified cases of Greenland sharks attacking divers. Untreated Greenland shark meat is toxic to humans. The Greenland sharks skin is very thick just like the sleeper sharks skin.

These sharks are affected by climate change, which is causing the temperature of the water to rise. Rory and Eyana were briefed by their boss about the expedition they were going to be going on.

I'm going to send a cooler along with both of you, so that you can collect samples of the ice and snow. I want you to log the temperature up there every day, and the water temperature.

> "Are we allowed to take a weapon with us just in case we have a run in with a polar bear?"

"Yes."

I'm going to take my best camera with me, so that I can take pictures of the animals up there.

I'm hoping that we see a snowy owl, they're my favorite animal. Make sure that both of you stay warm up there, we'll be just fine. I checked the arctic weather app and it said that it was in the negatives yesterday.

We're going to take the hand warmers that you got us for Christmas last month, we're going to use them very sparingly.

Chapter 2

If you have any issues or concerns you can call me anytime while you're up there. I have extra matches if you need them, we're definitely set in that department.

"Do you think the coats that you have are going to be warm enough up there?"

"The coats that we have are rated for negative degree weather."

A military helicopter is going to take you up there, along with some equipment.

"What kind of equipment are we talking about?"

"An amphibious vehicle, three large gasoline cans, a hardened foldable shelter, first aid kit, firestarter, flares, sample baggies for the samples, and 9 thermoses full of water."

"Would you like me to pack you some survival food?"

"No," thanks we'll figure out the food situation.

We packed crackers, 3 packs of beef jerky, a pound of cooper cheese, 2 smoked filets of salmon, 6 mini peanut butter sandwiches that we made ourselves. You're making me hungry talking about food, but still, you both eat healthier than I do.

I'm a big fan of cheese and baloney sandwiches, with a bag of chips. Neither one of us rarely eat potato chips, I think they taste too salty. While they were talking a massive 15-foot-tall elf with a beard rose up out of the depths in the arctic. His name is Quinta.

Legend has it that it's been frozen in time for a century. A snow witch casted a spell on the giant elf, after it came after the witch because she put a spell on his family and caused them to be sent into another dimension. The spell that was cast on the elf caused him to turn into stone and sink to the bottom of the sea.

He felt that he was free at last and was glad not to see the witch. When he stood up to walk he spooked several polar bears that were nearby. There was a man driving his snow machine, when he saw the giant elf he quickly got out of there. The giant elf rubbed his hands together, and many massive flames came up out of his hands. This caused the icicles all over his body to melt off, and his soaked beard dried off.

His skin turned back to an emerald, green color, and his blue eyes twinkled. He spoke words of enchantment, to heal his damaged soul. Then many penguins came walking over to him, hello my dearest little friends. We have a lot to do together, I must go off on my journey now.

The Penguins continued following him, suddenly the elf stopped walking. I must make you birds fly before we can continue our journey, hopefully I remembered the flying spell correctly.

Flya, fuma, guka, menimo, susso. The Penguins bodies spun around twice, and their eyes blinked many times, they were now able to fly.

The leader Penguin was able to speak, Quinta I don't think that you should go on the other side of the mountain.

The mermaid minotaur's will attack you again, I don't care because this time I'm going to defeat them once and for all. I'm going to use different tactics this time to attack them, yes I like you're thinking.

The monsters must be defeated and when they die they'll be sent back to hades, where they belong. There was a giant shark under the ice just waiting for the opportunity to attack the elf.

We're going to come under attack shouted the leader Penguin, keep moving. When an enormous shark slammed its head up through the ice, the elf punched the shark in the mouth with his massive fist.

The elf quickly grabbed an ice boulder, and slammed it into the shark's head, killing it. I doubt that's the only giant shark around here said the leader Penguin.

I still haven't figured out how you have become so fearless, and imaginative that's because my family taught me that.

A tear ran down the elves face, my family meant the world to me now I doubt I'll ever see them ever again.

The leader penguin flew up by the elf's neck and hugged him, I'll always be here for you, you never need to worry.

Once we're by the mountain, we won't have to worry about the sharks attacking us anymore. I don't think that you need to carry the ice boulder anymore, I'm carrying it just in case another giant shark attacks us. You must be very hungry by now; I am. The elf went over and grabbed the shark and took a bite out of it.

A few minutes later they reached the mountain, the elf quickly scaled the mountain, and was now at the other side of the mountain. A mermaid minotaur brought out its horn and blew it alerting the rest of them.

Just a short time later the rest of them showed up, and the elf and the penguins showed no fear of the minotaurus. The minotaur's were holding they're cursed curved blades and large shields.

The elf easily towered above the minotaur's, all the Penguins huddled up together, this was one of their lines of defense.

One of the 5 minotaur's ran at the elf, it only came up to his calf. One thing that the minotaur is good at is jumping up into the air. When the minotaur jumped up at the elf, he smacked him with all his might.

The minitour fell back hard onto the ice, just fighting one of them was bad enough, then another one made an attack on the elf.

Now back with the team, perhaps both of you should bring a board game with you. Besides that, we'll be too busy observing the beautiful animals, then playing a silly game.

I don't tell many people this but when I turned 30 years old, I learned how to play chess, my stepfather taught me.

It took me a week to fully understand how the game was played, and somehow I was able to remember all the names of the pieces on the board.

A year after that my stepfather became ill, so I stayed at his place for a while. His leg muscles became weak, and he could barely stand up anymore. He told me about the good times that he had with his buddies.

> "What did he do for work before he got ill?"
>
> "He was a fisherman, and always liked to tell me tales about the ocean."

He tried telling me that mermaids were real, and that there were mermaid minotaur's that would drag fishermen off their ships and wrap them up in cursed chains and let them sink until they drowned.

He said that if you saw a minotaur you never looked in his eyes or you would burn up. He told me about that tale when I was 18 years old, and to this day I've never forgotten it.

The next tale that he told me was even crazier than that one, he told me that there was a monstrous winged creature under the ice somewhere in the arctic.

> "How many times did your dad visit the arctic?"
>
> "3 times."
>
> "Our next question would be what in the world was he doing up there?"
>
> "He visited an Inuit friend of his."
>
> "Did he tell you how much time he spent up there?"
>
> "Yes."

He said that he spent 4 long days and nights up there and told me that he saw many animals. He said that he saw 2 bald eagles hunting together and showed me the many pictures that he took of them.

> "Did he see any polar bears up there?"
>
> "Yes," he saw four of them.

Before he passed away he gave me several books full of pictures, that he had taken of wildlife throughout the years.

Chapter 3

One of the pictures in the books were of a family of polar bears, I'm going to frame that picture and hang it up on my wall in my living room.

> “Do you have many pictures of your stepfather and you together?”

> “Yes,” and every time I go through them I get teary eyed.

He had a great wife, who took good care of him for many years. In his lifetime he owned 6 dogs, that he cherished very much.

Him and I always used to watch car racing, I took him to 8 different tracks around the United States.

He didn’t like riding on airplanes, so I would give him a book to read to calm his worried mind. He was very much of an avid reader. He preferred to read nonfiction books, and motorcycle magazines.

He had a 2012 Harley super glide, that he enjoyed riding over the weekends with his wife. They went to Japan, to see mount fuji which is 3,776 above sea level.

Then they went to see the 3 other holy mountains. On their next trip, they went to London, and did some sightseeing around the capital. The next day, they went to parliament hill, where they shared a glass of wine together.

They packed their things up and headed to the drone rental shop, where they rented the best-in-class drone and bought a SD card they put in the drone. They flew the drone around 2 historic areas, before it ran out of battery. Afterwards they took it back to the shop and went on with their day.

He was very much into traveling, and also enjoyed woodworking. A long time ago he had started up a wood carving business that thrived for a long time.

Many customers would come to his shop every day and some liked to watch him do his work. One of his customers came to him, asking him if he could carve a design into his rifle stock.

He willing did it, and that same year he completed designing 7 wooden stock designs for rifles. He never had a single person complain about his work, and some people gave him tips.

One time a duck hunter came to him asking him if he could make wooden light decoys for him. Him and the hunter talked it over and decided to make them out of plastic.

The hunter paid an extra to hurry along the process of making them. In just a few weeks he completed them, the hunter was so happy with his work that he told his hunting buddies about him, which brought him a lot more business.

"Did he have his shop on social media?"

"No," he was very old school and didn't like computers.

Meanwhile in Los Angeles, an artificial intelligent missile defense system was hacked and went haywire.

The engineers did everything that they knew to stop it, military officials were informed about the incident and they told the governor that he needed to get to his bunker as soon as possible. The governor was taken from his home and escorted to his vehicle, by his security guards.

The driver quickly sped down the street, and the governor bumped the back of the driver's seat. You're going way too fast; we may flip over going around the next corner.

Keep your comments to yourself and just let me drive. I know these streets better than most people do. My job is to get you to safety as soon as possible, just hold on back there and try to stay calm.

The security guards sitting in the back rolled down the windows and brought out there guns. While the governor just kept to himself, get ready everyone we're going to go down the street where the drug dealer is probably going to shoot. You think after being arrested 5 times he would have stopped shooting at people driving by.

Plus, two days ago when we went down this road one of you shot him in the leg, but I doubt he'll ever learn not to shoot at us again.

While they were going down the road the drug dealer didn't come out, when a man wearing blue jeans with a black hoodie took out his gun and started shooting at them.

The bullets bounced off the four-inch armor plating all around the car, the guards opened fire, causing the man to retreat back inside his residence.

They put their guns away and rolled the window back up, when they turned onto the next road they were faced with another dilemma.

There were at least 50 tents along the sidewalk and in the middle of the street, and there were people smoking joints in the middle of the street.

One of the people was playing the guitar, while he was doing drugs. Many empty aluminum soda cans and garbage was lying along the sidewalk.

Traffic was becoming backed up behind there vehicle, another homeless person picked up the cans and started throwing them at their SUV.

The guards jumped out of the truck to assess the situation, they walked over to the car directly behind them and knocked on the driver's side window. The woman rolled down her window, with a surprised look on her face.

"Are you a police officer?"

"No," I'm part of the governor's security team.

"What do you need me to do?"

"I'm going to need you to back up in a couple of minutes."

"Then he relayed to the rest of the drivers the message, sir what's going on in the street over there?"

"Homeless people and people on drugs are blocking the street with their tents."

"Has this ever happened to you fellows before?"

"No," this is the first time that we've experienced this.

The other security guard is currently talking with the people in the street, hopefully he can come up with a resolution soon.

"Do you really think that those people are going to do what he says for them to do?"

"No," I highly doubt it myself.

He better be careful what he's saying to them or asking of them because they could become violent at any time.

I doubt they'll become violent because they're too stoned to do anything anyway, that's a good point that you have there.

"How long have you been doing this kind of work?"

"For 15 years."

I enjoy my job very much, I'm sorry to cut you off but I'm going to check on my partner.

"How's it coming over here?"

"Not as well as I thought it would."

They're all refusing to move their tents and themselves out of the street. My patience is starting to wear through, I talked to the driver and he said that we're just wasting time trying to talk to these people and make them move out of here for us.

Chapter 4

Suddenly a large pickup truck came flying around the corner. The driver saw this and shouted get out of there at the top of his lungs, the guard on the right side of the street jumped out of the way. But the guard on the left wasn't so lucky and was struck by the truck and thrown up into the air.

The other guard immediately took out his phone and dialed 911. He told them exactly what had happened and they said that they were sending out an ambulance.

He bent down and checked him for a pulse, there was one, but it was on the weak side. The tents were run over by the truck and the people that were standing in the street laid there motionless. Then gunfire erupted in the street, it was the driver of the truck doing the shooting.

> "Weren't you going to take care of the shooter asked the driver,
>
> "No," because I have to take care of my partner.

I could fire you for not tending to a direct threat, get over there and get him. He wasn't sure of the whereabouts of the shooter, then the shooter stepped out into the open.

He noticed that the shooter was wearing a bulletproof vest, he fired hitting the man in the knee knocking him down. After the man was down he crawled out of the way, hoping to be able to escape.

The guard followed him and shot him one last time at point blank range. He made his way back to the truck and saw that the ambulance had just gotten there. He greeted the emts, with a hello. As they were pushing the stretcher into the truck.

> "How are you doing today Sir?"

> "Not so good because this is my partner here that got hit by an out-of-control vehicle."

I'd stay here and talk with you some more but we have to get him to the trauma center as soon as we can.

The EMT got in the truck and they took off. The guard got into the truck where the governor was so terrified that he was shaking.

The cars that were behind the SUV backed up allowing him to turn around, and he sped down another road.

> "What are you going to do about all those dead bodies left in the street back there?"

> "I'm going to call the coroner and the health department of California after we have arrived at the governor's bunker."

I saw what happened to your partner. It was traumatizing, hopefully he's going to be able to pull through. The way he looked after getting hit I doubt it.

Eventually they were able to get to the governor's bunker, the guard opened the door to the bunker and led the governor inside.

The governors cell phone went off, and he answered it on speaker. This is the Department of Defense letting you know that it's second missile defense system is going haywire. It fired 3 missiles off and struck the capital of Los Angeles, causing a lot of collateral damage.

> "What did the military engineers tell you caused this to happen?"
>
> "They're currently still looking into it."
>
> "Thanks for informing me, I have to go bye"

The guard sat down in the chair beside the governor. Suddenly the governor stood up and pointed out the window, there's a cougar roaming around out there. Don't worry about it we're safe here, I'm not allowed to shoot it anyway. I suggest that you call the Game Commission and see if they can come out to tranquilize it. After 2 hours the threat was over and the governor was driven back to his home.

Back in Greenland, the boss and the biology team finished their conversation when an incoming missile struck a few yards away from the building that they were in. It caused a quake knocking things off the walls and shaking everyone up.

Their boss ran outside to investigate what was going on out there, I think that we better go out there to. You can go out there, but I'm staying here. After several minutes their boss came back into the building.

You both won’t believe what I saw out there, I found a piece of a missile just yards from this building.

I'm sure both of you want to get back to your homes, and you're free to go if you'd like. Tomorrow at 9 o'clock, you'll have to meet your pilot at the airport and be flown directly to the arctic.

I'm going to stay here for another hour to see if anything else happens. Have a good night, thanks you as well. They both got in their cars and drove for an hour before reaching their homes.

Their evening went by way too fast, and before they knew it they were driving to the airport the next morning.

They made it to the airport 6 minutes early, the pilot was standing next to the military helicopter smoking a cigarette.

“Hello Sir, how are you doing?”

"I'm doing good."

They loaded up their luggage in the helicopter, the pilot dropped his cigarette and joined them. You can strap yourselves in a while, the pilot got in the cockpit and started up the helicopter.

I've been piloting people all over the world for many years. Minutes later they took off, 2 hours later they reached the arctic. The pilot helped them to unload their amphibious vehicle among many other things.

Thank you for all your help Sir oh you're welcome, good luck on your expedition. The pilot started the helicopter and flew out of there, the first thing that we should do is set up the shelter.

We're going to set up the shelter 50 feet away from here, alright. A snowy owl flew over their heads, we're not here 10 minutes and we've already seen some wildlife. Rory put his rifle over his shoulder.

They quickly brought out their camera, but they had already missed their opportunity. Eyana began working on putting the shelter together, stop looking around and help me with completing this shelter. I can't push hard enough to get these two parts together; you made that look easy.

A few minutes later they completed the shelter, I'm glad that job's done.

"What are you doing taking the caps off the gas containers?"

"I'm making sure that they're all full, you're just wasting your time."

Eyana gathered up all their food, placing it in the steel anti animal container. While Rory was checking out the amphibious vehicle, Eyana came walking over to him.

This vehicle has awfully big tires on it, I wonder how fast this thing can go. We must find the sat phone, Rory opened a small storage container and began going through it.

Eventually he got to the bottom of the container and that's where the phone was. Great job on finding the phone, Eyana went to work on preparing both their backpacks.

Rory took a piece of cheese out of the food container and ate it. 15 minutes later she was done putting together everything in the backpacks.

Eyana had the sample baggy in her hands, Rory bent down and picked up some snow. He was going to throw the snow at Eyana and saw 2 rodents run by him.

He thought to himself I hope these rodents don't get into our food while we're away." Eyana got a sample of snow.

Chapter 5

Rory saw another rodent but chased it away from their camp. Eyana walked back to the camp and saw Rory doing some kind of awkward movement.

> “Have you been practicing dancing while I've been gone?”
>
> “No,” I'm chasing away rodents.
>
> “What were you doing?”
>
> “Getting a snow sample.”

You should come with me when I get an ice sample. They headed out looking for an ice sample, I hope that one of us doesn't fall through the ice.

I'm scared to think about what's lurking under that ice, oh just forget about it. They soon came upon giant tracks; I didn't know that there were giants walking around up here. Eyana took out her camera and took a picture of the tracks, then they began following the tracks.

I'm just hoping that this thing doesn't come after us, we're going to make history if we find this thing. They soon grew tired of following the tracks and went off on their own way.

Look there goes an arctic fox, you have good eyes for wildlife. I'm getting tired, let's go back and get in the vehicle.

Half an hour later they got back to their camp and jumped in the vehicle, I'm glad that this thing is enclosed and has heat.

As they were driving along they saw a herd of reindeer off to their right. They went on much further and saw a lone muskox, this is rather odd to see them alone.

2 1/2 miles later, they came to a scene that petrified them. They saw the elf battling with the mermaid minotaur's. Don't move or they're all going to see us.

Minutes later they saw a few flying penguins, what we're seeing here is astounding. Eyana took out her camera and snapped a picture of them, then took several more pictures of the giant elf and the minotaur's. Suddenly the ice near the elf broke apart, and a massive, winged creature came up out of it.

The creature spotted them and flew their way, they quickly turned the vehicle around and got out of there. Eyana took the rifle off of Rory's back and fired it at the winged creature.

This made the creature fly away from them, a giant shark came up through the ice exactly where they were, throwing them and the vehicle in the air.

The vehicle came back down wheels down, Eyana got a concussion and a gash on her forehead. Rory hit his elbow.

The elf finished up defeating the last minotaur and noticed that the Penguins were gone. The elf headed to an area called safe, this is only a safe place for the elves.

Rory and Eyana drove 1/2 hours back to their camp. Eyana brought out the sat phone, and dialed emergency services. 10 minutes later a helicopter flew in and took them to a hospital in Greenland. All the equipment was left behind.

A week later they were discharged from the hospital. They called up their boss and told him what had happened, he was completely blown away about their story. A week later they resigned from their jobs, they searched for a better job and eventually found one.

www.ingramcontent.com/pod-product-compliance
Lightning Source LLC
LaVergne TN
LVHW052112160826
845678LV00015B/3499
* 9 7 9 8 3 6 9 8 9 1 1 7 9 *